CARTOON NETWORK™

THE POWERPUFF GIRLS

MOVIE

Saving the world before bedtime!

Adapted by Tracey West from the storyboards by Craig McCracken,
Lauren Faust, Don Shank, Charlie Bean, and Paul Rudish

Based on "THE POWERPUFF GIRLS," as created by Craig McCracken

WORLDWIDE PUBLISHING
WB™

SCHOLASTIC INC.

New York   Toronto   London   Auckland   Sydney
Mexico City   New Delhi   Hong Kong   Buenos Aires

Special thanks to Bethany Dixon, Allison Kaplinsky, Peter Koblish, Annie McDonnell, Sophia Psomiadis, and Amy Rogers for making this book possible

ISBN 0-439-38128-2

Cover and interior illustrations by The Thompson Brothers
Designed by Peter Koblish

12 11 10 9 8 7 6 5 4 3 2 1   2 3 4 5 6 7/0
Printed in the U.S.A.
First Scholastic printing, July 2002

The city of Townsville! Once upon a time, it was a sad and gloomy place. Criminals ran wild. Evil ruled supreme. The people of Townsville had no hope left . . .

. . . except for one man. Professor Utonium wanted to bring something good into the world. He mixed sugar, spice, and everything nice. As his curious lab monkey watched, one last ingredient made it into the mix —
An accidental dose of Chemical X!

There was a burst of light, and three perfect little girls appeared.
Professor Utonium was stunned. "What — what are your names?" he asked.
"You made us, so you should name us," said the red-haired girl.
So Professor Utonium named them Blossom, Bubbles, and Buttercup.

The Professor's girls were full of surprises. They were better than perfect. They had superpowers!

Blossom, Bubbles, and Buttercup flew around the house. They used super-strength to lift heavy boxes. Professor Utonium watched the girls in wonder. But someone else was watching, too . . . someone sinister.

The next day, Professor Utonium took the girls to school.
"Welcome to Pokey Oaks Kindergarten," said their teacher,
Ms. Keane.
Blossom, Bubbles, and Buttercup made new friends right away.
All the kids liked them.

At recess, a boy named Mitch Mitchelson taught the girls how to play tag.

"I'm It," Mitch explained. "All you have to do when you're It is tag someone else!"

Blossom, Bubbles, and Buttercup figured out the game fast. But thanks to their superpowers, things quickly got carried away.

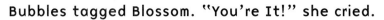

Bubbles tagged Blossom. "You're It!" she cried.

The girls zoomed through the school yard, chasing one another. They didn't realize it, but their game of high-speed tag tore up the school!

Blossom, Bubbles, and Buttercup were having fun. They chased one another into the heart of Townsville. They tore through the town like a triple tornado!

"You're It!" yelled Blossom.

"No, you're It!" Buttercup shouted.

The girls chased one another all over the city. Soon Townsville was in shambles.

"Who are these horrible little girls?" wailed the people of Townsville. "Why are they doing this to us?"

Ye Olde Townsville Crier Tribune News

BUG-EYED WEIRDO GIRLS BROKE EVERYTHING

Finally, Professor Utonium stopped the game. He took the girls home and tucked them into bed.

"Girls, I don't think you should use your powers in public anymore," he told them. "Your powers are very . . . special. People might not understand them."

The girls were confused. They didn't understand why people wouldn't like their powers. But they wanted the Professor to be happy. "We promise, Professor," they said.

As Blossom, Bubbles, and Buttercup slept that night, they forgot all about their game of tag.

But the rest of Townsville didn't.

The kids at Pokey Oaks Kindergarten were angry with the girls for messing up the school.

And back at home, the police came and arrested Professor Utonium!

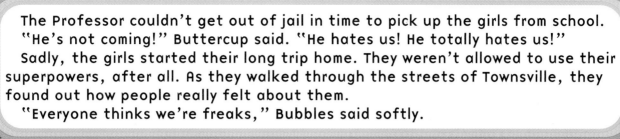

The Professor couldn't get out of jail in time to pick up the girls from school. "He's not coming!" Buttercup said. "He hates us! He totally hates us!"

Sadly, the girls started their long trip home. They weren't allowed to use their superpowers, after all. As they walked through the streets of Townsville, they found out how people really felt about them.

"Everyone thinks we're freaks," Bubbles said softly.

"Oh, well," said Blossom. "It couldn't get much worse."

But then it started to rain. The girls ducked into a dark alley — and were attacked by a gang of green bullies!

Then suddenly, out of nowhere, a garbage can lid came flying. The gang was defeated. But what mysterious stranger had saved them?

The girls found their hero hiding in the darkness.
"Thanks for saving us," said Blossom.
"Yeah, you rock!" said Bubbles.
The stranger stepped out of the shadows. "No, I do not rock.
For I, Jojo, am a freak!" he said. "I don't fit in anywhere."

Blossom, Bubbles, and Buttercup were not afraid of the strange-looking monkey.

"We're freaks, too," said Blossom. "We understand."

Then Jojo the monkey told the girls all about a plan he had to make Townsville a better place. The girls agreed to help.

"Maybe everyone will like us again," said Bubbles.

Jojo made the girls promise to keep their plans a secret.

So every night, while the Professor thought they were asleep, Blossom, Bubbles, and Buttercup flew out to help Jojo build the Help-the-Town-and-Make-It-a-Better-Place Machine.

They dove into a fiery volcano to harvest its energy. They used their superstrength to lift heavy beams. They even brought Jojo some Chemical X from the Professor's lab!

PRIMATES →

Finally, Jojo finished building his special machine. To reward them for their hard work, he took the girls on a trip to the zoo.

Blossom, Bubbles, and Buttercup had fun. But Jojo seemed very interested in the monkeys and apes there . . . maybe too interested.

That night, the girls tried to hide their excitement from the Professor. They couldn't wait for everyone to see Jojo's machine.

But back in Jojo's observatory, something sinister was happening. Jojo used the machine to transport all of the monkeys and apes to his lab. Then he zapped them all with Chemical X!

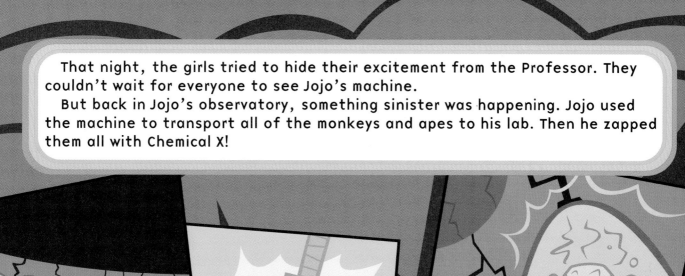

The next morning, the girls took Professor Utonium downtown to see the surprise. They were very excited. But to their horror, they found Townsville overrun by menacing monkeys and attacking apes!

"I am not Jojo, a mild-mannered monkey," Jojo cackled. "I am **Mojo Jojo**, and soon my fellow apes and I will take over the world!"

"But the machine was supposed to make Townsville a better place," said Blossom.

"It is a better place," Mojo Jojo replied. "For ME! And I couldn't have done it without you girls."

"You horrible children!" wailed the people of Townsville. "This is all your fault!"

"This wasn't supposed to happen!" yelled Buttercup. "You've got to believe us."

Professor Utonium looked sad. "I don't know who to believe," he said.

"Noooo!" Blossom, Bubbles, and Buttercup cried.

They flew up into the sky. The girls didn't care where they ended up — just as long as they got out of Townsville. Finally, they landed on an asteroid floating in space.

Buttercup was so angry that she started kicking rocks. Blossom tried to blame her sisters for what had happened. And poor Bubbles just cried.

Back in Townsville, Mojo Jojo smiled with glee as the super apes tore up Townsville.

"We will rule the world!" Mojo yelled. "And I will be king!"

The other apes didn't like the sound of that. They all wanted to be king, too. Soon the shouts and cries of angry, fighting apes filled the air.

"I, Rocko Socko . . ."

"I, Hota Wata . . ."

"I, Hacha Chacha . . ."

"I, Koko Kongo . . ."

"I, Baboon Kaboom . . ."

With their superhearing, the girls could hear the screams of Townsville citizens, even on the asteroid.

"What should we do?" Bubbles asked.

"Nothing!" snapped Buttercup. "Those people hate us. Why should we help them?"

Suddenly, Blossom, Bubbles, and Buttercup heard a familiar cry.

"It's the Professor!" the girls shouted. They zoomed down to Townsville to save him.

The girls tried to find the Professor, but they couldn't. And wherever they looked, they saw people in trouble.

Bubbles was the first to make a move. She scooped up a woman before she could be crushed by a falling beam.

Blossom and Buttercup followed their sister's lead. Soon all three girls were saving people from the mad monkeys.

"I know how we can stop the monkeys and save the Professor," Blossom realized. "We can use our superpowers!"

Bam! Buttercup's power punch sent Rocko Socko flying.

Slam! Bubbles made a jump rope out of the Go Go Patrol.

Wham! Blossom turned the tables on Baboon Kaboom.

The girls kept attacking until no monkey or ape was left standing.

Blossom, Bubbles, and Buttercup had defeated the apes, but their troubles weren't over.

While they were fighting, Mojo Jojo took Professor Utonium to his observatory. The girls flew after them.

As they watched in horror, Mojo Jojo gave himself a superdose of Chemical X. Then he grew . . . and grew . . . and grew.

"Now I am mo' Mojo than before!" bellowed the giant monkey.

27

The girls flew the Professor to safety. But now they had another job to do.

"We have to fix the problem we helped start," said Blossom. "Girls, we've got to stop Mojo!"

The girls did their best. They hit Mojo with every punch and kick they could. But Mojo wouldn't give up. He gripped Blossom, Bubbles, and Buttercup in his strong hand and carried them to the top of a tall building.

"Join me, girls!" Mojo Jojo said. "If we work together, we shall rule!"
The girls used their last ounce of strength to break free from Mojo.
"We won't join you because we are stronger!" yelled Blossom.
"Because we are invincible!" yelled Bubbles.
"Because we have the power!" yelled Buttercup.
The girls pummeled Mojo. Then together they gave him one big push.
"And because you are IT!" they yelled.
Mojo toppled off the tall building. Professor Utonium quickly gave him an
antidote to Chemical X, and Mojo turned back into a normal-sized monkey.

"You can give us the antidote, too, Professor," Blossom said.

"Maybe everyone would like us more if we were normal," added Buttercup.

"No!" cried the people of Townsville.

"Your powers are awesome," said the Mayor. "You were all flying and running and punching and then BAM! It was so cool."

"Would it be okay if we called on you sometimes to, like, save the day or whatever?" the Mayor asked.

Blossom, Bubbles, and Buttercup couldn't believe it. That would make them so happy!

"Can we, Professor?" they asked.

Professor Utonium thought about it. "Well . . . okay. As long as it's before your bedtime," he said.

31

And so, for the very first time, the day was saved, thanks to The Powerpuff Girls!